Seers & Salt

A Woodside Cosy Urban Fantasy

Melissa Gunn

ROSE KOWHAI PRODUCTIONS

ISBN ebook 978-1-0670066-3-1
ISBN paperback 978-1-0670066-4-8
ISBN audiobook 978-1-0670066-5-5

Contents

Author's note

This book is written in New Zealand English. It may contain more 'u's and 's's than you're used to.

Chapter One

I didn't plan to run a magical bookshop. No-one does, surely? My plan was to move to the city and get a regular job, leaving all the expectations of being a sibyl in a long line of sibyls behind, along with my family. In case you didn't know, sibyls are traditionally messengers of the gods, or seers. My ancestors provided the words for oracles. In modern times, my family still provides forecasts. For a fee, of course. But it's not that they were mean or nasty — they're not gorgons or anything like that. It's just that it felt like I had to live up to family expectations every single day. And I was failing.

That failure really hit home when I lost my dog. No, he didn't die. He disappeared while I was visiting a farm owned by a distant cousin (a farmer with a sideline in animal-feed predictions), after I failed my final sibylline test. Studying helps with everything except giving actual prophecies, it turns out. I went to the farm to restore my equanimity after my failure, but in the end, it was the worst thing I could have done.

Out on the farm, there were so many places for Rex to disappear. Shearing sheds, feed sheds, the upper mountain, the neighbouring farms. We searched, but the verdict was he'd either been dognapped (he was a handsome German shepherd after all, and there were lots of other farms nearby), or had gone off after a bitch in heat. Not one of the seers in my family pinpointed his location, and I was eventually forced to return home, broken-hearted and alone in all the ways that counted.

"He's gone where he's needed most," my aunt Helen said after a long scrying session.

Not what I needed to hear. After the years I'd spent with him as my companion, losing Rex was a big deal. I'd trained him as a puppy when I was a teen, laughing at his gangly legs and huge paws. I'd groomed his long Alsatian coat and walked endless miles with him as an adult. In so many ways, I sensed that losing him was a turning point for me. I couldn't stick with the sibylline lifestyle any more, not least because I'd flunked the test, but mostly because of losing Rex. If the thing I loved most in the world could be lost and not Seen, I didn't want to be a part of that world. Something had to change.

"I know you miss Rex, but you can get another pet," my mum told me.

"Look at it this way, you don't have to get a sitter for your holidays now," my dad said.

"Why don't you get a cat?" my sister said.

"Get yourself a bird," my friends said. "How about a talking parrot?"

Well-meaning, all of them, but missing the point.

"I just want to get away," I told them.

My mum was silent for a few moments. "Your aunt Helen has a cottage at the beach. Why don't you take a week there? Then you can get back to work with a clear heart and mind."

I crossed my arms. Now it came to the crunch. I hadn't been enjoying working in the family business since well before Rex was lost. I'd put off working for the family firm for as long as possible by spending years in online grad school, but since I'd finished there, I'd had no excuse not to join in, even without my sibylline certificate. At least, no excuse they'd accept.

Since then, I'd been hand to the grindstone, trying to pull my weight in a business I wasn't suited for. So, it wasn't only Rex's loss that had been weighing me down.

"No, really away. It's time for a change. I've got my degrees, I don't want to do any more school, and I *don't* want to go back to making stock predictions."

Mum gasped.

Dad said, "Now really, Sibyl, you can't mean that."

"But we always have more work than we can keep up with," said Delphine. "Even with your help doing the background checks. Why would you leave?"

Delphine is my younger sister. She had the same curly dark brown hair and tan-to-golden skin as me but was five years my junior, and she always managed to get the easiest jobs in the family business.

"Why?" I demanded angrily. "Because I don't *want* to spend my entire life getting up early for the overseas exchange openings, reading the financial papers to see if the family's predictions are correct, and dealing with boring, boring stock markets!"

As I said, sibyls are traditionally prophets or seers. And for the last century, my family has been using their abilities to provide financial planning services. The trouble is, I'm not much good as a prophet. Hence, having to read the financial papers. Instead of seeing clear visions of the future, I've spent my whole life trying to gather enough knowledge to act like a prophet without actually being one. Despite spending all day, every day, with my head stuck in grimoires, histories or advanced calculus lessons, I'm a failure. The only one in a family of hereditary seers who can't *see*, at least not the way they do.

Of course, I'm the one who got stuck with the name Sibyl, while my sister, with her native ability to receive messages from the gods, got named after the site of the oracle in Greece. Unlike her, I have to accumulate knowledge the hard way and think my way through things, like mundane humans. I have to do *maths.* Most of my family do a bit of a trance, maybe some automatic writing, and voilà, predictions for the client. If I try a trance, I just waste the day. Automatic writing? A bunch of meaningless scribbles. I haven't once had a genuine prediction or sight. It probably doesn't help that I've never had *any* interest in stock markets. But I haven't received the wisdom of the gods about anything else, either. If it wasn't for my ability to make minor wards and charms, I'd think I was a mundane. As it was, I knew I was a dud as a seer. And I was sick of trying to pretend otherwise.

"It's time for me to stand on my own two feet," I told them all. "I'm well overdue for a holiday at the very least. I'm heading away, and no-one is going to stop me."

They looked at me, then Dad raised an eyebrow at Mum. I wondered what unspoken message he was passing, but I didn't have to wonder for long.

"I told you she'd do this," Mum said to Dad.

"I suppose you don't want to borrow a suitcase," Delphine said.

If I'd been ten years younger, I would have stamped my foot. It's so typical of my family that she didn't offer to *give* me a suitcase. Perhaps they've been rich for too long; they don't like to spend money on anything.

"No, I do not. I've bought my own backpack and bus ticket." I checked my phone ostentatiously. "In fact, I had better go now so I don't miss my bus. Bye, all."

They burst out into a cacophony of protests and questions.

"But you can't just leave!"

"Where are you going?"

"What about tomorrow's market briefing?"

Ignoring them all, I stalked to the back door, where I'd stowed my backpack.

"I don't care about the briefing, Mum. You'll all do better in the business without me, anyway."

Mum blinked at me, at a loss for words.

Dad spoke. "Your attitude is highly irresponsible, Sibyl. The firm relies on you to show up for work."

Gee, thanks for the family love, Dad.

"But if you go, *I'll* have to do the briefing," Delphine complained.

"We'll see how you're getting on," Mum said.

I was sure they would. Seers, you know. But with that sort of send-off, I didn't think I'd be telling them my side of any events. Their lack of understanding made a dull weight in my stomach as I heaved my backpack on and shut the door behind me. They did love me, I was certain. But in recent years they'd seemed blind to the fact that I was struggling to keep up, sacrificing all my spare time to the job. For the family.

I'd had enough of putting family first. Now it was time for me. And that's why I set off in my late twenties with only what I was able to carry on my back, ready for an adventure.

Chapter Two

I wasn't late for the bus. It would be at least an hour before any bus turned up. I watched the ducks chase water sprites on the pond near the main road while I waited. I found myself torn between hoping someone from my family would follow me and tell me how much they needed me to stay, and being fiercely glad that I was doing this on my own. I'd definitely stuck around at home for far too long. Why hadn't I headed out on an adventure as soon as I reached my majority? It must have seemed like the right thing to do at the time, to remain at home and support the family business, but present-me was kicking past-me.

Should have left long ago, Sibyl.

When the bus pulled up at last, wheels crunching on roadside gravel, I was more than ready for it. Not one of my rather large extended family had bothered to come by and persuade me to stay, or at the very least, see me off. That cemented my decision. Yes, I'd stormed out. And sure, they were probably checking out my future in crystal balls, scrying pools, mirrors, or even the backs of their own eyelids. My family is nothing if not diverse in their methods of seeing. But none of that translated to a proper send-off, and I secretly wanted them to wish me well.

I shouldered my backpack again and paid the fare in cash. Despite what I'd told my family, I hadn't bought a ticket in advance. My plan had been to take whichever bus showed up first. North or south, it didn't matter. All that counted was going away. And it's harder for seers to predict the future if there's a lot of uncertainty in it. I didn't want them to know *everything* I was doing. I had decided I'd go to one of the bigger cities. Everyone says there are more opportunities in the big city.

The bus was heading north. I decided that was a good thing. I didn't need more frost in my life, and the northern city of Auckland, Tāmaki Makarau, was subtropical since we lived in the southern hemisphere. Despite all my time studying maths, I had to count the change twice before I had enough for the long trip to the city. Advanced calculus doesn't help with making change when you're a bundle of nerves.

The only free seat on the bus was next to an old lady who told me her life story twice before we'd reached the edge of town.

"And that's how you ended up all alone in the world except for your niece," I said along with her the fourth time she told me.

She grinned gummily at me.

"Have I met you before, dear?" she asked.

I wasn't sure if her eyes twinkled as she said this, but I'd been brought up to assume the worst and do my research before believing the best.

"I don't think so," I said. "But the story seems familiar somehow."

She broke into a wheezing laugh, her eyes crinkling up so much they disappeared into her wrinkles.

"Good on you for being polite to an old woman," she said when she'd got over her laughing fit. "My memory isn't what it was. Now, I tell you what, I could do with a bit of a kip. How about you be a good girl and make sure no-one steals my bag between here and the city?" She patted the bag between her feet. It was large, with odd bulges, and had a bookshop's logo emblazoned on the side of it — an open book with what looked like the sun coming up over it, the whole enclosed in a circle. Under the sun and book was a slogan, 'Find your magic'.

I gave her a polite smile. "Sure, I can do that," I agreed. After all, how much trouble could that be? I'd done my research for both directions of travel, and I knew that there were only a few stops between my town and the city, none of them long. Plus, if she thought her bag was safe, she might doze off and forget to tell me her life story for a fifth time.

"Don't let anybody touch it, mind," she said as she folded up an extra cardigan and propped her head against it.

"I won't," I promised. Sure enough, a few minutes later, the only sounds from the old lady were ladylike snores.

The first sign that guarding the old lady's bag wasn't going to be the walk in the park I expected came while I was trying to make a list of what I should do when I got to Auckland. I'd got as far as 'find accommodation' when I noticed a curl of smoke wafting under my seat. My immediate thought was to pull the communication cord on the bus and yell fire, but this smoke was purple. I looked around. In front of me, a couple of leprechauns sat on cushions to raise them high enough to see out the windows.

"In a meadow, there lived a cow named Lou,
With spots so big, they looked like goo."

They were entertaining each other with a poetry slam competition, and it didn't sound like either of them had the attention or skill to send a smoky tendril out at the same time. I ruled them out almost as soon as I heard the first line.

Spread across several seats over the aisle, there was what looked like a sports team, nine or so lean, toned, individuals who were probably still in school. They wore matching singlets in pale blue and were in constant motion, changing seats, leaning over the backs of the seats to talk to each other, and laughing hysterically at the leprechauns' poems. They were far too busy laughing to be the source of the smoke.

A grizzled older man yelled at them to keep the noise down from time to time, but otherwise ignored them, despite wearing the same singlet. On him, the singlet highlighted a developing paunch and long underarm hair. He appeared to be deeply concerned with the sports pages of the folded newspaper on his knee. Also, surely I'd see the trail of smoke crossing the aisle, if he was the source. I turned to look behind me. Most people back there seemed to be asleep. I looked at each of them in turn, suspicious that someone was faking it.

The back seat was full of werewolves, or so I guessed. We didn't have werewolves in my home town, Te Pōhue, but I'd heard about them. There were rumours that they competed with hunters out in the hills. Most of the werewolves on the bus had long hair and beards, but there was one that was actually in wolf form, laughing at something one of them had said in a doggy way. I looked away hastily; he reminded me of Rex. I hoped Rex was having a fun time out on the farm, and not having to spend too much time protecting his new master while my cousin made his dull predictions. I shook my head, bringing myself back to the present. Everyone knows werewolves don't *do* magic, since their inherent magic is tied up in transformation. Smoky trails were not going to be within their purview.

I looked out the window for a moment, not sure how I'd trace the smoke. We were passing through a darkly forested valley at this point, and I caught sight of my own reflection in the window of the bus. Curly, dark chestnut hair dominated my face, even with my glasses on. On humid days it gets frizzy, but this was a good hair day and it lay flat at the top. I have the grey eyes that go with seeing in my family — the reason I'd been given my name. In the glass they looked silver. I hated my eyes. They were a reminder, every day, that I looked the part of a seer without being able to fulfil the expectation.

Only my torso showed in the glass; I was too short for anything else. A lot of the bus reflected in the window too. It looked like there was an empty seat behind me. Odd. I hadn't noticed an empty seat earlier. I turned away from my reflection and saw that I must have been mistaken; there was someone in that seat after all: swathed from head to foot in clothing, a hood covering their head, and dark sunglasses covering their eyes. It could have been the dark background that made them blend in. Unless they were a vamp, of course... No, surely a vamp wouldn't catch a public bus in the middle of the day? I shifted uneasily, and the person turned their covered head to look at me inquiringly. The purple smoke didn't even pass underneath their seat. "Nothing," I muttered, and hastily looked away.

A couple of seats ahead of the leprechauns, a massive figure took up both seats on one side of the bus, dreadlocked red hair falling onto huge shoulders. I'd passed the troll while looking for a seat. He'd been asleep then and was probably still asleep now. Unless the old lady had ore in her bag, it was unlikely the troll would be interested. Besides, trolls aren't known for their abilities with magical smoke, so despite his intimidating appearance, *he* probably wasn't the culprit.

I decided the best way to identify the source of the questing smoke was to follow its trail. I could pretend to visit the bathroom at the back of the bus. That would give me an excuse to head back there. First, though, I should make sure the inquisitive smoke didn't find anything. After a moment's consideration, I threw my jacket over the old lady's bag. Before I left home, I had packed a bunch of things — herbs, crystals and ornaments from my room — into the pockets of my jacket. Hopefully, some of the items should deter the smoke. Holding on to the metal handles on the edges of the seats, I unsteadily made my way towards the back. I looked carefully at each face as I passed — well, apart from the covered face of the possible vamp. But mostly I was following the smoke. I was only two seats away from the crowd at the back when I noticed it drifting out from another bag. This one was on a seat beside a wizened-looking man who was wearing a woolly hat with a pompom on it despite the warmth of the day. He had his eyes closed, but a gleam of darkness at the bottom of his eyelids made me think he wasn't sleeping.

I tried to play it polite. "Sorry to bother you," I said. "But is it your genie investigating my friend's bag?"

The man opened his eyes and stared at me. His dark eyes looked like pools of black tar in the relative dimness of the bus, and I shivered, wondering if I had been wise to disturb him. What if he was a wizard in disguise? They are legendarily quick to anger, though not usually renowned for their pom-pom hats.

Then he glanced down at the tendril of smoke and a smile cracked the stern lines of his face. He gave a wheezing laugh.

"Get back here, you rascal," he said.

I blinked stupidly for a moment, before realising he was talking to the smoke. He batted the bag with a dark, age-spotted hand, making a dull, metallic clunking noise where it hit the fabric. There must have been something inside it — probably a teapot or vase, if the smoke really was a genie. As I watched, the purple haze coiled up on itself like a movie played backwards. It condensed into a tornado-shaped spiral, then sucked itself back into the bag.

"Now behave, or I won't let you out when we get to the city," the man said. This time, I was sure he wasn't speaking to me, because he leaned over the bag as he spoke, directing his words into the gap the smoke had disappeared into. There was a small puff of purple smoke, as though in acknowledgement.

The old man looked at me again and blinked slowly. "Djinns," he said in explanation. "They're worse than cats for curiosity."

"Isn't it dangerous carrying a djinn around in your bag?" I asked. Djinns have an even fiercer reputation than wizards.

"Oh, I've given up worrying about that," he said, not reassuring me at all. "Besides, him and me are old friends now. And he's safer than a vampire. More likely to grant wishes than try to suck blood, or souls, or anything nasty like that."

"That's good," I said, taking a step back. The bus lurched as it went over a pothole and I had to grab at the seat beside me to stay upright. "So, um, can you keep him from getting into other people's bags? Only I don't think my jacket will keep a djinn out for long."

He shot out a hand and grabbed my wrist. I gasped at the sudden invasion of privacy. Then I gasped again as the bus crested a sudden rise and almost flew down the hill that followed, leaving my stomach behind. We hit a pothole and I was sure the bus left the ground on the other side of it.

The old man's grip on my arm was all that kept me on my feet. Out the window, I could see that the road ahead had a steep drop to a river on one side, and a rocky cliff face on the other. The pothole had sent us far too close to the drop-off. And as we veered wildly across the road, I saw that half the lane was missing where an earlier landslide had sent the asphalt surface into the ravine.

The bus driver took the corner too fast, then hit the brakes hard. The bus tilted ominously towards the drop-off as the brakes screeched. My heart thundered in my ears as I stared into a ravine that seemed like an abyss. I held my breath, wishing I had levitation magic as the drop loomed closer.

I've only just started my journey. I'm too young to die!

Gasps and screams sounded around me as others clearly had the same thought. I stumbled forwards exactly at the moment that the purple smoke of the djinn shot through the window as though it wasn't there. It looked like it clung to the cliff face for a few seconds, acting as a drag anchor, spreading itself wide and thin. Were those smokey purple fingers scrabbling for purchase on the rock face? As we rocketed around the corner I found myself noting every blade of grass and aspiring shrub growing from crevices in the rocky cliff face in excruciating detail, filtered through a thin lilac haze, as though memorising such things would save me. Then the moment passed. The bus slowed down, its dangerous tilt correcting itself. As we drifted away from the emptiness of the cliff edge, the screams of the other passengers died away. My own throat felt rough from a cry I hadn't known I'd released.

When we were finally travelling at a pace that seemed more reasonable for the terrain, the smoke curled back into the man's bag once more.

"He'll stay in for now," the old man said, releasing my arm as if nothing had happened. "Unless our fool of a driver tries a stunt like that again," he added with a frown.

"Let's hope not," I said lightly, as though I hadn't just about ended up in the lap of a stranger while our bus plunged to a rocky end in a ravine. I loosened my suddenly clammy hands from their death grip on the seat handle.

That would never happen to any of the rest of my family. They'd see it and avoid the trip.

In fact, couldn't one of them have warned me?

I felt a frown forming on my own face as I thought about my family. Why *hadn't* they warned me? Then again, I've often been told that seeing isn't an exact science, especially when there are random variables which can change the future dramatically. That's why the family is only comfortably well-off, rather than billionaires. And why I was able to fake it for a while with hard work and study, even if that hadn't paid off in the long run. That was also a big reason behind my decision to catch the first bus that came along, instead of planning my trip in detail. More random variables to throw my family off. All the same, life without a family of seers warning me about every possible event was going to be very different. I hadn't realised how different until that moment.

Chapter Three

POETRY PAIN

As the ride smoothed out, the bus emerging from the steep-sided gorge into wide, rolling downs, I forced myself to relax. I was on an adventure, and no-one was going to ask me for a prediction on stock market futures anytime soon. I smiled at the old man.

"Thanks for keeping your djinn in check. And, um, thanks to him for keeping us on the road, too."

A tendril of purple smoke snuck out of the bag and wrapped itself briefly around my wrist.

My skin tingled — not unpleasantly — where it touched. Then it withdrew, and the bag looked once again like an old, well-used piece of luggage.

"Anytime, young lady," the old man said. He grinned at me, displaying a set of teeth that looked far too white and complete to be real at his age. "Perhaps him and me can drop in on you once you've settled in."

Not another seer. I almost groaned aloud.

The old man chuckled at my expression. "No, no, that's not a prediction," he said. "I don't have that skill. But I've been around long enough to recognise someone seeking their fortune when I see them."

I nodded, hoping to strike a balance between acknowledging his words politely and not being too encouraging. I wasn't at all sure I wanted an old man and his djinn as accomplices in my new life.

A bark from the back seat grabbed my attention. The werewolf in wolf form that had been sitting between the hairy fellows there was now standing on the seat, looking out the back window, tail wagging enthusiastically. It was difficult to see through that window due to the painting that covered the back of the bus, but I managed to distinguish a group of cows standing silently in a field. A small boy was sitting on the top rail of the wooden fence near them with some sort of musical instrument in his hands. I squinted at the rapidly receding herd, wondering why the werewolf had been so enthusiastic. The big white cows did seem to have a bit of a glow to them.

One of the human-form werewolves barked back at the wolf.

"Get down, Dirk," he said. "You know we can't touch cows."

"'Specially not those cows," another werewolf growled. "They're the cattle of Helios, the lot of them. We'd have no end of deity-driven trouble if any of us turned a hair on their hides."

The bus crested a hill, and the cows dropped out of sight. The werewolf, Dirk, gave a disappointed whine and sat back on the seat. The werewolf who'd identified the cows as sacred to the Greek sun god gave Dirk an approving pat. He must have felt my stare, because he looked up at me.

"Looking for the loo?" he asked.

I nodded. It had been an excuse before, but after the scare with the cliff, it was a need now.

"Too bad, there isn't one on this bus. Hope you can cross your legs for another..." he glanced at his watch. "Another twenty minutes. There's a rest stop in Rotorua."

"Thanks," I said. After all, that *was* my cover story. If only I didn't feel so embarrassed about it. I gave a big fake smile and hurried back to my seat.

The old lady was still asleep, despite the squeals of the sports team and the lurching of the bus. I retrieved my jacket — after all, I'd been assured that the djinn wouldn't intrude again — and searched its pockets for my own timepiece. I don't like wearing things on my wrists, so I rely on my phone for timekeeping. The werewolf had been right about the time until the next stop. And while I hadn't needed the bathroom before tracing the purple smoke to its source, now twenty minutes seemed like an eternity. Every pothole was cause for concern. I needed a distraction.

Luckily, distraction wasn't far off. The troll up front suddenly reared up out of his seat and twisted around to face the leprechauns.

"Enough poetry!" he roared.

The leprechauns clung to each other, their matching hats bumping together.

"But it's all in fun," one of them said.

"We'd only just begun," said the other.

"We could make one for you," the first one said.

I wasn't sure if that was a threat or a promise. But the troll clearly viewed it as a threat. He gave a wordless roar of rage.

Heedless of his own safety, one of the leprechauns launched forth.

"There was an old troll on our journey,
Who wanted the end to come early,
But when all's said and done
We were just having some fun,
And nothing the troll said could deter me."

As the leprechaun proclaimed his limerick, the troll's large hands gripped the seat back harder and harder. Just as the leprechaun finished the last line, the troll's fingers broke through the vinyl seat cover with a crackling, tearing noise.

The bus driver glanced in his rear-view mirror. "No damaging the bus," he called in a stern voice. "Or you'll be walking."

"Can't. Stand. Poetry!" the troll snarled. "Stop!"

I had to agree with the troll's sentiments, at least in regard to this particular poetry, although I wasn't going to take out my feelings on a public bus.

"Have it your way then," said the leprechaun. He seemed to think he'd won something, having said his piece without incurring troll-inflicted damage to his own person. He turned to his companion. "Have you got an audiobook? I could do with a little relaxation, don't you know."

The second leprechaun fished out a small audio device.

"To be sure, I've got three loaded here."

"Why didn't you say so sooner?"

The troll narrowed his eyes at the brazen pair, but they ignored him, and within seconds, were snoozing on the seat with earbuds in their ears.

"Humph," the troll snorted. Then he slowly turned around and lowered himself into his damaged seat, folded his arms, and appeared to go to sleep.

"Everything alright back there?" the bus driver called back, apparently happy to intervene now that all had been resolved.

Chapter Four

Brief relief

The bus passed several steaming hillsides — evidence of geothermal activity — as we made our way into Rotorua. Almost everyone alighted for the 'rest stop' when we arrived. My snoozing bus-seat neighbour awoke with a snort when the bus lurched to a stop, brakes hissing. She grinned gappily at me.

"No problems with my bag then, dear?" she asked.

I hesitated a moment before answering, trying to figure out how best to word things. "Just an inquisitive djinn," I said. "He's agreed to leave your bag alone now."

It was hard to miss the way her hands clutched at the bag when I said that, especially when she heaved the bag onto her lap. It was obviously heavy. Given the bookshop logo, maybe it had books in it. But it wasn't the usual sort of book bag. More of a heavy duffel. With a padlock. My mind set to work on the puzzle. I'd figure it out sooner or later. That's one thing about all the degrees I've earned — they've given me a good brain for working things out. Even if I'm not so good at acting on what I learn. But here I was, escaping my family, ready to reinvent myself. Perhaps I could learn to act on things too.

"A djinn, eh?" But she didn't say anything more, simply stood up when the aisle cleared enough for us to leave the bus. "Hurry up, dear, there'll be a queue for the necessaries and you won't want to miss the next stage of the trip. There'll be some proper fortune-seeking opportunities then. I'm Kath, by the way."

"I'm Sibyl." Then I wondered if I'd missed an opportunity to give myself a new name.

The way Kath spoke sounded exactly like one of my family, with their clairvoyant abilities. I wanted to retort that perhaps I might want to stop here to find my fortune instead. But I realised in time that she was probably just being kind in an old-ladyish way, rather than making a prediction. After a lifetime spent with a family of seers, I was hyper-vigilant about predictions.

In any case, Rotorua is renowned for its assorted dragons and taniwha, which, while exciting, wasn't what I was looking for in my fortune-seeking. Even from the bus stop, I could see steam rising in the near distance from some geothermal site. Typical swamp dragon territory. We don't have dragons in my hometown; it's too cold for them.

I shivered. I'd read all too many stories about dragons and their propensity to eat people. Also, cats, small dogs, and the odd ground-nesting bird. I *didn't* want to encounter a dragon of any type. My reading had suggested that dragons cluster at geothermal sites, using the hot ground to keep their eggs warm while they hunted. They liked to nest in places where the boundaries are thin. Boiling mud pools, where the heat of the earth and the dampness of water combine, are their favourite. I shuddered at the thought. I had a deep-seated fear of dragons, thanks to my risk-averse upbringing and excessive reading habit. No, I definitely wasn't planning to seek my fortune here. I'd seen videos of boiling mud too, and it wasn't something that enticed me at all. I simply hoped we'd steer clear of both dragons and mud during this short stopover.

Outside the bus, the troll was waiting while the bus driver retrieved his bag from some inner storage compartment. The leprechauns had stayed on the bus. I was rather disappointed by that – I'd already heard enough of their poetry efforts for a lifetime – but at least they and the troll wouldn't be clashing over poetry on the next leg of our journey.

I hurried to join the predicted queue. Kath came too, her bag pulling her over to one side with its evident weight. Idly, I wondered again what she had in there.

"Tell me more about this djinn you saw," she said as we waited. "Did you meet its carrier?"

Djinns almost always have carriers: someone who moves their bottle, lamp, teapot or other vessel around in the world. Unless you meet them in a treasure cave or some such, which is what happens when they *lose* their carriers. It does sound like a perilous existence, relying so much on someone else. I supposed djinn-carriers were fairly motivated. The usual legends abound with stories of wishes granted to djinn-carriers. I read a fair few wish-fulfilment stories in between maths extension classes, back when I was at school. I brought my focus back to the old lady.

"Yes." I told her about the pom-pommed wizard, and how the djinn had prevented the bus from plunging headlong into a deep gorge while she was asleep.

She laughed uproariously at my description of the wizard.

"I'll be sure to tell him the pom-poms match his style," she cackled. "Silly old git, he didn't want that hat when I first gave it to him."

I felt my eyebrows lift in surprise.

"You know him then?"

"Know him? I'm married to him."

When the old lady had stopped laughing at my expression, I asked politely, "Why weren't you sitting together, then?"

She patted my arm in what I had to admit was a rather condescending way. "Move along, dear, the queue's getting shorter."

We both shuffled forward a couple of steps, then she continued.

"When you've been married as long as we have, you take the opportunity to meet other people. Also, that djinn annoys me no end. He's into everything!"

I snorted. That was certainly true.

"I thought he was going to steal something," I admitted.

"He probably was, dear. Like I said, he's into everything. Worse than a toddler! It's your turn."

When I emerged, there was no sign of the old lady. Kath, I supposed I should think of her. I checked the time on the big clock. I should have enough time to purchase something from the tea-room by the bus stop before it was boarding time again.

There was a queue in the tea-room, too, and it looked like the other passengers had already raided the baked goods section where I automatically headed. The only things left behind the plate-glass-protected stand were a thick piece of ginger slice and a lonely-looking custard square. In my home town I'd have picked the custard square every time (at least, I would if my home town actually had a tearoom, instead of a pub that got destroyed every time it was rebuilt. My family had made a few prophecies warning against the rebuilds, but they'd been ignored as such prophecies often are). But something made me hesitate. I was on an adventure, re-inventing myself.

Try something different, a little voice inside my head told me.

"I'll take the ginger slice, please," I told the server.

She nodded and smiled, placing the heavily iced slice into a small brown paper bag for me. I used cash to pay for my purchase, thinking that I might give my seer relatives a harder time to track me if I didn't use the banking system for just a little while.

I hurried outside with my slice, hoping to get some fresh air before the bus left again. Fresh-ish, anyway. The air in this town was scented with sulphur. The bus driver sauntered into the tea-room as I walked out, so I was fairly sure I'd have the chance to eat, before I had to board the bus again.

I was brushing the last crumbs of ginger slice off my shirt — it had been surprisingly good, with its combination of fierce heat and overly sweet icing — when a shadow passed overhead.

Just a gull, I thought. The shadow wheeled and returned, and I glanced up from my seat on the brick edging of a raised garden. *A pigeon?* It was definitely something winged. And sort of grey, with iridescent lacing around its neck. It was coming in fast though, and I wasn't in the mood to be a perch. I stood up. That's when I noticed the djinn's purple smoke drifting around my feet. Its disembodied voice hissed in my ear. I hadn't realised it was able to talk.

"Duck!"

Almost too late, I realised that it wasn't advising me of the presence of a waterfowl, but issuing an instruction. What I had thought was an innocent, if much-maligned dove, was in fact a small dragon in pigeon colours. And it was hurtling towards me with its mouth open and claws extended. As it grew closer, I saw that it was at least twice the size of a real pigeon, and its wide-open mouth was emitting yellowish steam. Not as scary as smoke, perhaps, but steam scalds are extremely painful.

I ducked.

As a result, the dragon skimmed over my shoulder, snagged a claw on my hood, tearing it slightly and leaving a smear of mud, and landed in the flowering bushes in the raised garden. One ear felt warm where the dragon's breath had got a little too close for comfort. Leaves showered everywhere, some of them singed and smoking. I wrinkled my nose at the smell — which told me I'd been in this town for long enough to stop smelling its pervasive sulphuric odour.

A warbling coo emerged from the shrubs, along with a gust of steam which brought back the sulphur smell in full measure.

"It wants food," the djinn advised me.

"I ate mine!" I said in panic. "What will it do if it doesn't get food?"

"Eat something that isn't food," the djinn said. "Like you. Or more likely your bag, first. Dragons aren't picky eaters."

Great. I hadn't even made it past my first outing in a new town, and here I was being threatened with death-by-dragon.

"It's too small to eat me," I pointed out in what I hoped was a reasonable voice. My fingers tightened around the straps of my backpack. I'd sacrifice it to save my life if I had to, but it contained everything I'd thought worth bringing from my old life. I wasn't prepared to give it up without a fight.

"Dragons have those unhingeable jaws," the djinn explained — not very helpfully. "A bit like snakes, really. They can widen them to get around pretty much anything that stays still."

"I don't think I'd stay still if a dragon was trying to eat me."

"Not unless their breath had knocked you out first," said a new voice a little way behind me. I turned my head just far enough to identify the speaker. It was the pom-pom wizard, the djinn's carrier. "That's why it smells so bad. Too much of the stuff will put you out like a light."

"Why in Gaia's name did anyone think it was a good idea to import dragons?" I asked, only sort-of rhetorically. They really did seem like the sort of pest no-one should have even considered bringing into the country.

"I expect for the same reasons they brought sparrows and rats," the wizard said. "There's nothing quite like the pests of home."

I took a cautious step backwards, hoping I wouldn't fall over the djinn. I wasn't sure how corporeal his smoke was. "I'm trying to get away from the irritations of *my* home," I said. "I'm not interested in being eaten by someone else's pests."

The dragon emerged from the bushes. Now it was on the ground, it moved a lot slower. I could see its leathery hide, and the prettily coloured pink-and-green-on-grey scales that decorated its head and neck. They merged into its body almost seamlessly. It filled up its chest and emitted another coo. It was definitely pigeon-adjacent. The earth melted where it stood, and little boiling mud pools erupted where the earth was damper, next to the watering system. I doubted anyone would want to have a flock of dragons in their backyard, any more than most people want pigeons around. The dragon twitched its tail sideways, touching a watering hose just long enough to melt a hole in it. Water sprayed out, turning to steam where it hit the dragon. Before long, the dragon was invisible in a cloud of evil-smelling steam.

"Now would be a good time to run for the bus," the wizard remarked. "Assuming this isn't the last stop of your journey."

Someone nudged me with an elbow and I almost screamed, thinking the dragon had snuck up on me. But it was Kath, clutching a brown paper bag like the one I held, oil already leaking through from its contents. She put her locked duffel bag at her feet.

"Don't believe everything a wizard says, will you?" she said. "There'd be no living with dragons if they were as bad as he makes out. I'll just give it this and we'll be on our way." She pulled a meat pie out of her paper bag and paused with it in her hand. "Hmm. Do you think it wants it with sauce or without?"

The djinn sent a tendril of smoke towards the pie, only to be batted away by the old lady's other hand. "Not for you, you pesky thing. Sibyl here needs to know about the care and management of dragons in case she happens on them again. If you want a pie, go manifest one." She cackled a little. "With sauce, I think," she said. She tipped a small plastic sachet of tomato sauce out of the bag and handed it to me.

"Open this will you? And be quick, the dragon's got the scent now."

She was right — through the steam, large nostrils were flaring wide.

"Only because you're mucking around with sauce," interjected the wizard. "And pies are cheating." He looked aggrieved. Perhaps he'd had some fancier, more wizardly way of dealing with dragons.

I hastily opened the sauce sachet. "Um, where do you want it?" I asked. Meat pies were a thing I saw other people eating, not something I ate myself.

Kath whipped a small wooden fork out of the paper bag, dug a hole in the pie pastry and proffered the pie. "In there will do nicely, dear. Makes it easier to throw cleanly."

I squirted the red sticky liquid into the damaged pie. As soon as I'd done so, Kath hurled the pie directly into the steam. The dragon's head popped out long enough to engulf the pie (demonstrating its unhingeable jaw in the process) and disappeared back into the steam.

Kath carefully wiped her hand free of any pie pastry, popped the paper pie bag in a nearby bin and picked up her heavy-looking travel bag.

"Right," she said. "*Now,* we walk at a moderate pace towards the bus, suitable for old ladies. Once we're behind metal, we can report the sighting and have the proper authorities deal with it. No need to get involved, is there, Ron?" She directed her last words at the wizard. Then she turned and walked away from the dragon, the djinn, and the wizard.

The wizard, Ron, looked a little sheepish. "Better do what she says. Dragons don't digest pastry well, so that pie's not going to stay down long. It won't pay to be nearby when the inevitable happens." He looked at the djinn, which was still wafting around me. "You'd better come along too," he said. "You're not doing anyone any good where you are."

The djinn contrived to look sulky, drooping in coils.

"Alright, thanks for saving her from the dragon," Ron said, apparently understanding its meaning without words. I wondered why it didn't talk now when it had before. But it swirled away towards the bus before I could ask.

I followed it hastily, not wanting to be scalded, eaten, or party to the effects of pastry on a dragon. Ron kept pace with me, pom-pom bobbing gently, and waved me on before him in an old-fashioned, gentlemanly way.

Most of the passengers were already on the bus, except for the werewolves. I wondered if they were stopping here in Rotorua, or if they were continuing on to the big smoke like me. I found it difficult to determine my emotions about that. Their doglike nature reminded me painfully of Rex; their status as predators made me uncomfortable. But they'd been helpful — sort-of.

The bus driver swung himself onto his seat, depositing several brown paper bags next to him. "Everyone good to go?" he asked. He turned on the bus, which juddered to life, and reached out to press the door-closing button. Just as he did so, there was a bark, and a stream of werewolves in wolf shape bounded in. One of them shimmered up into human form, grabbing a long coat from beside the door of the bus and slinging it on.

"Sorry," he panted. "Ran by lake."

"No worries, mate," the bus driver said agreeably.

The rest of the werewolves padded down the aisle to take the back seat again. The human-form werewolf gave me a nod and a smile as he walked past.

As the bus pulled away from the stop, I looked out the window. A squad of people in full riot gear had surrounded the flower-garden where I'd eaten my ginger slice. The dragon erupted from the shrubbery, flew into someone's plastic shield, bounced back, then took off, beating its wings rapidly. As its wingbeats swirled the steam aside, I spotted the sad remains of a half-digested pie. Though I was still terrified of dragons, I couldn't help but feel a twinge of sympathy for it. Poor dragon.

It headed off in the same direction we were going, passing in front of the bus before heading for the hills.

Beside me, Kath gave me a nudge with her elbow. "Better a pie than you, eh? Did I tell you about the time..."

I settled into my seat, more than ready for a less exciting journey.

Chapter Five

ELEMENTAL

Despite my unfortunate dragon encounter, I felt a pang of regret that I hadn't stuck around for a few days to explore Rotorua. I'd have to come back this way one day to do so. But only if I figured out a better way to protect myself from dragon attacks.

Kath seemed much livelier after our stop, so I took the opportunity to ask her how she knew how to deal with dragons. Partly, I hoped that would divert her from another reiteration of the story about her niece — which I had serious doubts about anyway, now she'd said she was married to the pom-pom wizard. She was hardly alone in the world.

"Well, that's a bit of a long story, dear," she said. "It was actually my niece who taught me the pie trick. Although I have to tell you, it only works on the sillier dragons. No matter how much they love pies, an experience or two like the one you saw teaches most dragons to avoid anything in pastry."

I shuddered. "Yes, I can see why. What was Ron — your husband? — planning to do? He seemed to think there was another way to sort out the problem." The main reason I wanted her to talk was to distract myself from the terror I still felt. Even now I could see that dragon's mouth opening wider and wider. I'd have nightmares about it, for sure.

Kath shook her head slowly. "Ron always thinks he knows a better way to do things," she said darkly. "He's got a soft spot for those dragons, see. Doesn't think I should be feeding them pies." She cast a sharp sideways glance at me. "They don't bother humans for food if you start with pies. They're fast learners, as a rule. One pie and a dragon will leave both humans and bakeries alone in future."

"I suppose that works," I said slowly. "Isn't it a bit cruel, though? I mean, I know how bad it feels to have gastro, and I wouldn't wish that on anyone. Not even a dragon."

Kath shrugged. "That's life for you. I could have been cruel by letting it eat you, of course. Then it would have been captured and put down, rather than simply rehomed to a dragon sanctuary in a suitable spot. Sometimes you have to pick your cruelty."

I looked out the window, uncomfortable with the idea, but not wanting to argue with an old lady who probably wouldn't change her mind, anyway. Plus, I was glad to have been saved, even if it *had* meant discomfort for the dragon.

This conversation wasn't helping me relax at all. We were passing through a strange, boulder-pocked area. Farmland surrounded small hills covered in giant boulders and remnants of native bush. Mist still wreathed some of the higher tors. Or was that smoke? It looked like there was a bit of red or orange under the mist.

I leaned forward, trying to make sense of what I was seeing, and bumped my nose on the window. Ow. I rubbed it self-consciously, hoping no-one had noticed my gaffe.

"What's got your nose, dear?" the old lady asked.

This could be more important than embarrassment, Sibyl, I told myself.

"Does that look like flames to you?" I asked, pointing to the nearest mist-and-tree-topped hillock. "Under the misty, smoky stuff?"

Kath leaned around me, squinting. She moved her specs from a chain around her neck to her face, looked again through the glasses, and nodded. "Definitely flames. Can you be a dear and pull that cord?" She pointed with a knobbly finger to the emergency cord that was strung along the wall of the bus from front to back.

"What could be causing a fire out here?" I asked her as I reached for the cord and gave it a yank. My yank resulted in a muted buzz near the front of the bus. Next thing I knew, the driver had slammed on the brakes and only my hand — still on the cord — was keeping me from being pressed forcibly into the seat in front of me. The screeching of the brakes filled my ears, along with a surprising variety of snarls and curses from the other bus patrons.

"Sorry," the bus driver called. "Is everyone all right?"

There was a chorus of 'yes', with the odd 'no' and 'maybe' thrown in, but it seemed that no-one had been badly hurt by our abrupt stop. Kath was probably the only one completely unaffected. When I looked, she was still sitting bolt upright as though glued to the back of her seat. As I watched, she muttered something incomprehensible and squirted something in a spray-bottle over her shoulder. Then she sat forward more normally and blinked at my startled expression.

"You have to be prepared for accidents," she said calmly. "These buses don't always have seat belts, so I always bring my own charm-stick and removal spray."

Easing my pulled shoulder back into place, I wished she'd offered me some of whatever charm-stick was, earlier.

My home town was clearly more backwater than I'd realised. I was learning a lot about the world I hadn't known, and I hadn't even reached the big city yet. Speaking of which… "So, what are we doing stopping near a wildfire?" I asked. "Assuming it is a wildfire, of course."

"Oh, I doubt it is, dear. That's why I wanted us to stop."

"Who pulled the cord?" The bus driver had stood up and was looking sternly down the aisle of the bus, hands on hips.

The old lady got up creakily and stepped around a couple of members of the sports team who had taken advantage of the stop to practise hand-stands next to their seats.

"I asked my friend here to pull it," she said. "There's an outbreak of elementals in the boulders, and if we don't deal with it now, it'll turn into a major incursion."

I shook my head at her. Surely it was the job of farmers or firefighters to deal with problems in farmland, not a random assortment of passengers on a bus trip.

"I know what you'll be thinking," she said sharply. "You'll be thinking it's not your problem. But it *will* be your problem if we ignore it and carry on our merry way. Elemental incursions don't just go away. They spread. An incursion here could turn into a major incident if it's not nipped in the bud. We're talking highway closures, air pollution over the whole country, cities burnt to the ground."

I swallowed past a sudden constriction in my throat. *What if I hadn't seen the flames?* It didn't bear thinking of.

"I'll deal with the elementals." The pom-pom wizard, Ron, stood up, glaring at his wife. The djinn wreathed around one of his arms. "You always make such a drama about them, when you and I both know that all that's required is a simple rain spell."

"I know no such thing," the old lady declared, crossing her arms over her chest. "Every time you say that, and every time I have to help you out of trouble."

"You do not—" Ron began heatedly.

"Please, calm down, everyone," said the bus driver. "I have a schedule to keep here. If you want to go play with elementals in the bush, maybe you can catch the next bus?"

The wizard and the old lady both glared at the bus driver.

"I didn't *think* you had ambitions to be a toad," the old lady said. She unlocked the padlock on her bag using a key which hung on a chain around her neck, opened her bag and started rootling around in it. "Ah. Here we go." She pulled out a large grimoire, emblazoned with what was probably a Celtic knot, but could also be local carving. It was hard to tell when most of it was obscured by her hands.

Where did she find *that book?* I was impressed with its age and evident power, though I was certain she shouldn't be turning our bus driver into anything. I wanted to make it to the city, not get marooned in a forest. Plus, if an elemental incursion was as bad as Kath made out, we'd definitely need a getaway driver.

"Or you can provide me with a speed spell and a 'don't look' charm so we can catch up on the schedule without getting speeding tickets," the bus driver offered hastily.

The old woman nodded. "What a quick thinker you are, dear," she said to him. "That sounds like an excellent solution. Now, who else on this bus is good with elementals?"

There was a long silence.

"I *can* ask for volunteers one by one," she said. Somehow there was menace in the suggestion. "Of course, the longer this takes, the faster our driver will have to go to make up the time."

That was definitely a threat. I hated to think of the bus driver going faster around the bends than he already was.

One of the werewolves down the back of the bus stood up. "We can help," he said. The rest of the pack stood too.

"Very good," said the old lady. "Anyone else?"

One of the leprechauns cleared his throat and proclaimed.

"When the forest blazes, alight,

with a total lack of tigers bright,

you'll find that words flow slower than water,

not much use to stop the slaughter."

I groaned at the bad poetry. "If you're meaning no, you could have just said so," I told him.

"And what about you, Sibyl dear?" Kath asked me.

I felt myself flush. I *knew* I tended to sit back and let things happen, but that's a hazard of growing up with seers. If everything you do is already known anyway, why bother trying to change it? But I was trying my hardest to change, both myself and my attitude. I was convinced that being away from seers would bring about a better life, or at least a more unpredictable one. In any case, I wanted to get away from the continued refrain of 'I saw you were going to do that'. If my family were here, one of them would no doubt have seen the probable elemental incursion and avoided it somehow. But they weren't here, and I was. This was my chance to do something unpredictable. "I'll help sort the elementals," I said to Kath. "But you'll have to tell me how. I can just about manage a ward or charm, but that's all I have to work with."

The old lady beamed at me. "Well done, dear. I knew you could be proactive."

I hoped I hadn't just agreed to do something really stupidly risky. I didn't know much about elementals, except that they were dangerous, unpredictable, and that they showed up on the news from time to time as having caused some disaster or other. I look at the other seated passengers nervously. What did they know that I didn't? Still, I'd said I'd help now, and I stick to my word. I squared my shoulders. Somehow, I'd help. Surely, with a wizard and whatever Kath was along, we'd be alright? I still felt like a lead weight had settled in my stomach.

The purple smoky djinn snaked along the aisle of the bus and wafted along my arm.

"Does that mean you're helping too?" I asked.

"Yes. Elementals must go home," it whispered.

Well, having a djinn along was certainly going to improve our odds. Djinns were almost elementals themselves. The lead weight in my stomach wasn't quite so heavy.

Kath surveyed her team. "Come on Ron," she said, her voice crackling with command. "I'll let you have another go at renovating the bookshop if you help out."

So there really was a bookshop. I felt a zing of interest, distracting me from whatever mad thing I was about to do.

"You have a bookshop?" I asked. But I can't have asked loudly enough because no-one answered me directly.

Ron the pom-pom wizard made a grumpy noise. "It's you who wants it renovated," he grumbled. "But I'd better come along or you'll probably do everything backwards and confuse our young friend." He made his way to the front of the bus. "And no driving away without us," he added to the bus driver. "I've put a hex on the engine in any case. My bags are on this bus and they're not arriving in the city without me."

The bus driver opened his mouth, then closed it again. Perhaps he *had* been planning a getaway.

"Just don't be long about it," he said at last. "My schedule..."

"Yes, yes, we understand. Your schedule doesn't allow for saving the world. That's *our* job, isn't it Ron? And you can join in today, Sibyl dear." Kath beckoned me to follow her and made her way off the bus, still carrying her bag.

All the werewolves followed us, including the one called Dirk. The ones in human form were predictably hairy; the one in wolf form had more-than-usually human eyes, but was otherwise indistinguishable from a large dog of the wolfy variety. I thought of Rex with longing, but it would be crazy to try to pet this one the way I would my dog. None of them said much as they filed off the bus, though the human-shaped ones looked grim. There was certainly no tail-wagging, assuming werewolves did that. Apparently, an elemental incursion was no laughing matter. I bit my lip as I stepped off the bus. What had I let myself in for?

Once we were off the bus, I could smell smoke in the air. There was a wide stretch of grass before we hit the trees, and then some managed plantation forest before the native forest took over on the hill. Pine trees stretched out to the hill in even rows, their grey trunks blending into brown needle-covered ground in the distance. An occasional tree-fern provided a welcome splash of green relief to my eyes. But where we'd normally be taking a pleasant stroll, it now seemed as though something evil might leap out from behind every trunk. There were no bird calls, and the air felt hot and heavy.

"Let's hope those pesky elementals aren't too far in," Kath said as we hurried through the trees. "My knees aren't what they once were."

"I thought it was your hip that's been giving you trouble?" Ron said, trudging along beside her.

"That too. How are your ankles today?"

"They've been better."

Great, we're setting off to deal with fire elementals, up a hill, into a highly flammable pine forest, with a couple of old people who both have probable mobility issues. What could go wrong?

I strode forwards as fast as I could, thinking that I could at least give advance warning if I got to the elementals first. One of the werewolves padded up beside me, feet silent on the spongy ground. He had curly blond ringlets that bounced a little with each step as he walked, and deep brown eyes. He seemed friendly enough despite the general sense of urgency.

"We're faster," he said. "Can scout."

"Thanks." I didn't think I'd be able to manage a swift exit if I had to help both Ron and Kath escape in a hurry. "Have you dealt with elementals before?"

The werewolf paused for so long I began to think he wouldn't answer. But perhaps he was only choosing his words with care, because he suddenly said gruffly,

"Yes. Tricky." He raised his nose to sniff the air, then bounded ahead — perhaps to do the scouting he'd suggested.

That wasn't encouraging. I decided a werewolf would probably smell the elementals before me, and fell back to talk to Kath before we arrived at an elemental-versus-elderly battle scene. Not that the werewolves or I were elderly, of course. As we moved further from the bus, the air became thicker with smoke, and I covered my mouth with my shirt in an attempt to breathe without coughing.

"So, what do I need to do to help with these elementals?" I asked Kath, my voice muffled by cloth. "I haven't come across them before."

Kath was breathing heavily, but keeping up a good pace, and I abruptly felt bad that she was having to tramp up a hill at her age. She'd put a soft cotton scarf over her own mouth and nose, which must have made it hard to pant.

"You must come from a well-warded town," she said between rasping breaths. "They tend to break through where no-one's looking. It's a good thing you spotted this incursion before it got too big. Elementals can cause a lot of damage."

She must have seen my worried expression because she patted my arm. "Not to worry. I only need you to read from the book I've got in here." She swung her heavy bag. "I've lost my specs."

I looked at her in bewilderment. "They're on your face," I said.

"Ah, that'll be why this forest is a bit blurry. They're my reading specs." She removed the offending glasses and blinked around in apparent appreciation of her newly crisp vision.

"Um. What can I really do, then?"

"Don't worry, dear, I'll think of something."

That wasn't what I wanted to hear. I wanted to be brave and bold, but it was hard to do that when I knew nothing about what I was doing. Maybe I was overthinking it, but overthinking pretty much defined me.

"Can I read about elementals in your book while we track them down?" I asked.

"I suppose so, dear," she said, after a pause to look me up and down. "If you can read without bumping into trees."

"Oh, I can read anywhere," I said eagerly. "I used to read while I walked my dog, sometimes." Not that Rex had let me get away with that often — he wanted my attention on him, not on some slices of dead tree. Speaking of dead trees, there must have been a stand of them up ahead, because the quality of the light changed. I looked up, trying to see the difference. That's when I saw the fire raging down the hill towards us.

Chapter Six

The fire elementals were having a moveable feast-style party. At least, that's what it looked like to me, as they leaped from treetop to treetop, burning the uppermost needles before moving on to the next tree. Even from a few hundred metres away the heat was intense. There was no time to read about the elementals. They were almost upon us.

The sweat from our brisk uphill walk turned clammy on my back. I'd never seen a more terrifying sight. *Surely one of my relatives would have* seen *if I was going to be consumed by an elemental forest fire,* I tried to reassure myself. *Then again, maybe they did, and that's why they tried to get me to stay at home.* So much for reassuring myself.

"What are we doing here?" I asked in panic. "This is a job for a fire crew. With helicopters!" I didn't think I'd be able to get away in time if I ran from this fire — and I was sure that Kath wouldn't be able to, given her sore hip, knees, or whatever it was.

"Show her what you've got, Ron," Kath said.

Ron opened the bag he'd been carrying, and the djinn wafted forth.

"Couldn't you have warned me?" the djinn moaned, a whisper of sound that barely carried through the crackling of burning pine needles. Despite his words, he quickly expanded out of the bag, and we were shortly dwarfed by a huge, purple smoky being. The smoke from the burning trees mingled with the smoky djinn until it was hard to see where one stopped and the other began. Except that the elementals formed flickering, red-tinging-to-white shapes in the treetops. Every few seconds one would leap to a new tree, or another would lean down, mouth open wide to snatch a bite of burning pine needles.

"Ready to amplify on your mark," the djinn said.

Ron raised his hands in the classic mage-about-to-do magic-pose, and Kath put down her own bag and pulled out the grimoire.

"Here," she said, thrusting it at me. "Open it."

"Which page?" I asked frantically, taking the heavy book. I couldn't tell if the warmth of its covers was from some magical internal heating, from the elementals bearing down on us, or from sitting in a closed bag in the sun.

"Any page will do. Quickly now."

I opened the grimoire. It fell open somewhere just short of the middle of the book, on a page with a single line of text in a gothic, embellished script. I glanced uncertainly at Kath. Sparks showered down on us.

"Read it, girl," she said impatiently, scrubbing cinders off her steel-grey hair.

I read. "It says, 'In case of emergency, call upon thunder, fire or rain.'" I had expected some sort of spell or charm. This seemed more like common sense. I brushed a glowing pine needle off the book, leaving a smear of soot on the page.

"Well fire's not going to do it," Kath muttered. "Try rain, Ron," she called to the pom-pom wizard.

"Mark!" yelled Ron in a husky, old-man's shout.

"Mark," the djinn echoed in a booming voice that had pine needles showering down on us — fortunately, not yet burning ones.

Ron directed a watery bluish streak of *something* towards the elementals, who had reached the treetops only a few metres away. The djinn somehow bounced the blue streak around, like an echo of itself, before shooting it back to the elementals in a smallish wave.

At times like this I wished I'd been born into a wizard family. They really do have the most showy of the magic types. Kath hadn't done anything spectacular, but I suspected she could if she wanted to. Assuming she wasn't a seer, of course, but apart from that one comment back in Rotorua, she hadn't exhibited the usual signs. To my surprise, the water magic wasn't especially effective despite its showiness. The elementals hissed like embers when the water was thrown on them, and shrank a little, but that was all.

"Lay it on a bit thicker," Kath told Ron. "We'll work to contain it so it's more effective." While Ron flung his water-magic at the elementals again, she dug around in her bag and pulled out a pair of tongs, several paper packets of salt with the Rotorua bakery logo on them, and a truly enormous roll of duct tape. "Where are those werewolves?"

"We're here." The werewolves stepped out of the trees on either side of the elementals, both human and wolf-shaped. I wondered why they didn't all switch to one shape or another, but now wasn't the time to ask. "How can we help?"

"I'll need you to create a circle around the elementals with this tape," Kath instructed. The human-form werewolf took the tape with a nod, unpeeled the end, stuck the roll onto a piece of pine branch and gave the branch to a wolf-form werewolf who took it in his teeth and dashed off, pulling the duct tape out as he went.

Kath tore open salt packets and sprinkled the sticky side of the duct tape as it was pulled out. "Here, Sibyl, keep the tape flat for me," she ordered. "Follow that werewolf, sprinkle salt on the tape, and make sure you fix any tangles and tears."

I did so, reflecting that this was not how I'd expected to pass the afternoon. But the simple, though odd, task helped me to calm down. I had to keep pausing to adjust my shirt over my mouth, but I managed to apply salt to the entire roll of duct tape. The stuff stuck to my fingers and threatened to tear as the uneven gait of the wolf holding the stick with the roll on it made the tape jerk this way and that. Irritation at the growing stickiness on my fingers was a surprisingly good distraction from the roar of the elementals' fire which was growing larger to my left.

By the time the werewolf returned to Kath with the end of the duct tape in his mouth, I was in control of myself. Still scared, but no longer panicked. The werewolf was certainly faster on his feet than any human. The human-form werewolf completed the circle with the last sticky bit of tape. The stick that had been in the wolf-form werewolf's mouth was of course covered in slobber. Its legs were blackened with soot and it panted, lolling its tongue out. If I hadn't been terrified, I would have laughed at how similar werewolves and dogs were.

Chapter Seven

Circle It with Salt

Although the werewolves were fast, the elementals had closed the gap between us in the short time the werewolves and I had taken to make the duct tape circle. The sound of the fire they'd brought was overwhelming, not so much a crackle as a roar. Heat beat down on us. My hair began to crimp against my scalp. Pieces of burning pine needles fell from the canopy, sparking spot fires on the ground and singeing the bare skin on my arms.

I don't want to die this way.

I put my hand on Kath's arm.

"We'd better retreat!" I shouted over the din, then coughed, because I'd breathed in a mouthful of smoke when I inhaled to shout.

"Not yet," Kath snapped. "Open that book again."

Fairly naturally, I thought, I'd closed the grimoire.

"You're mad!" I didn't shout that though, I muttered it. Shouting insults at a witch or wizard would probably have meant certain death — even more certain than the threat posed by the elementals. I did take a large step back though, so my skin didn't quite blister. Then I opened the book, and this time I didn't wait to be instructed to read aloud the words I saw.

"Three times round the charm, quick or else you'll be quite warm." Despite my fear of the fire the elementals brought with them, I snorted at the odd rhyme, which required a weird, posh accent to make it work in any way. "This book might rival those leprechauns for bad poetry."

The grimoire grew noticeably hotter in my hand and I slammed it shut again hastily. There was a *lot* of lore about sentient grimoires and what they could do when miffed. Generally, they're safer to deal with when closed.

"Best be polite with it, dear, or it won't help next time," Kath said. "Now, you've read the instructions. Pass me the grimoire and off you go. Take the werewolves with you. They can make sure you don't get lost in the woods, and keep that dragon away too."

I felt my eyes bulge with shock. "You want me to run a circle around the elementals?"

"Well, you'll be faster than I will," she pointed out, not unreasonably. "And the werewolves alone won't do the job. Isn't that right, Ron?"

The wizard, still wearing his pom-pom hat despite the heat of the fire — or perhaps it shielded his head a little? — nodded.

"That's right," he said, voice cracking a little. "Werewolves don't carry the same metaphorical weight when it comes to elementals. Good with dragons, though. They give them the eye, you know, like sheepdogs and sheep. Don't worry, the djinn and I will distract the elementals with water while you do the job."

I hoped the elementals didn't understand English, or they'd know our plan. Perhaps it was fortunate that the roar of fire as the trees caught alight increased at that moment.

"Alright, I'll do it," I told Kath and Ron, hoping I wasn't sentencing all my hopes and dreams to a fiery end. I'd wanted to be a more proactive person, but this exercise seemed increasingly suicidal. Why hadn't I stayed safely on the bus with the other sensible people? And what if the dragon turned up while I was running in circles?

"Good girl. Take the extra salt with you in case you spot a break in the circle. The werewolves will help you make it round." Kath thrust a couple of paper salt sachets into my hand. I shoved them into my pocket and prepared to run. It was a good thing I wasn't a heels kind of girl, I reflected, as I tightened the laces on my sneakers.

While we spoke the wolf-form werewolves dragged fallen branches in their teeth and the human-form ones brushed a clear space in the pine needles, forming a sort of fire break, although the lack of any break in the canopy made me wonder if it could possibly work. The blond werewolf in human form caught my eye when I looked around for the clearest path to start my run.

"Ready?" he asked. His short blond beard was dark with sweat from the heat.

There was no doubt about it, werewolves really did have superior hearing. I hadn't thought any of them had been close enough to hear Kath's words.

"I suppose so. I'm not much of a runner though," I warned.

"Wait," the werewolf said.

"Do you mean for me to wait now, or you'll wait for me if I'm slow, or wait, this whole thing is just a nightmare and I'll wake up soon?" I asked tartly. The dicey situation was definitely getting to me.

"Yes," the werewolf said, grinning. Red elemental light glinted off his canines, making me shiver as he held out his hand. "Run, now."

It was a good thing he'd added the suggestion to run, or I might have forgotten my pacifist upbringing — seers are big on avoiding wars, including personal ones — and socked him one for his imprecise answer. Alright, I probably wouldn't have, but I certainly thought about doing it. I ignored his hand and took off, feeling like a less-than-graceful Bambi running through the burning forest.

The werewolves ran with me as I began following the outside of the duct tape circle, going widdershins since most spells and incantations called for that direction. It was a bit like running with a pack of dogs. Although I liked dogs, I wasn't sure that werewolves came into the same cuddly category. Racing through the woods with them was well out of my comfort zone, even beyond my fear of the elementals.

I slipped several times on the slick, sloping pine-needled surface, and once fell into a half-dug rabbit burrow on the side of the hill. But true to their word, the werewolves, even the wolf-shaped ones, waited every time I did so. I was only partly glad of that. A predator you can see is probably better than one you can't, right? Odd noises in the forest didn't help my frame of mind. There was a howling, growling scuffle just out of sight at one point. Werewolves facing down dragons, perhaps? But maybe that was the elementals. The fire they brought was causing a lot of noise.

It didn't take long to reach the charred zone where the elementals had passed by. Astonishingly, it looked like the fire they'd left in their wake wasn't taking; rather than charging into the flames as I'd half expected, the werewolves and I merely had to run (or lurch and stumble, in my case) through black and smoking trunks. It was still hot, and smoky, and I put my hand on an unexpected ember once or twice when I slipped on unburnt pine needles. But the circle also wasn't as large as I'd feared. I began to hope that we might survive after all. If I could just complete whatever twisted magic there was in following a triple anticlockwise circle of salted duct tape...

It was not the stuff of stories, I thought, as I slipped again and a human-form werewolf grabbed my arm before I could slip inside the elementals' circle. All the same, if I survived, the sound and heat of the elementals roaring in the treetops was sure to haunt my nightmares. From behind, they were practically invisible, but their effects weren't. I coughed, and ran, and coughed some more.

"One!" Kath cackled when she saw me coming down the hill. "Just two more to go. Keep distracting them, Ron."

The djinn was still bouncing Ron's wave around inside the circle. The wave made little hisses and emitted steam whenever the elementals came into contact with it. But it wasn't anywhere near engulfing the red-and-white, flickering beings that threw themselves around within the salt circle. Tree-trunks charred wherever they touched, and the heads of the elementals blended into the flames that crackled in the canopy. Elementals were not small.

"Hurry up, girl, I can't keep this up forever," Ron urged.

"Unlike myself, of course," the djinn added.

"That's what you think, you pretentious spirit," Ron muttered at the djinn. Despite the urgency of the task, the djinn took the time to be affronted, forming a more recognisable face in order to do so.

"I'm not a spirit, you ignorant wizard," he said, pausing to cross his wispy arms and look down his smoky, purple nose.

Don't stop to listen to a grumpy djinn, I told myself. *Even if that does sound like a proverb.*

A wolf-form werewolf dashed ahead of me, and the blond human-shaped one jogged a pace to my right.

"I'm coming," I panted. At least I wasn't doing this with my backpack, I encouraged myself as we started heading uphill again, leaving Ron and Kath behind.

Somehow, I'd imagined saving the world from an elemental incursion would be a little less physical than this.

My breath rasped in my throat and I couldn't keep my shirt over my mouth as well as run. My eyes stung and watered, every breath hurt, and all the while my imagination ran riot. What if the elementals escaped after all? How much of the forest would burn? Would it reach Rotorua? Would the bus and its passengers be able to escape, given Ron had hexed the engine? What about me and my dreams of freedom in the city? It was hard not to feel sorry for myself, but I kept going all the same.

Steam from Ron and the djinn's efforts mixed with the smoke and made it all but impossible to see as we went on. I slowed and peered through the forest, trying to spot grey duct tape through grey smoke. A werewolf yipped to the left of me, so I headed that way. After a few paces, I could see the tape again, winding through the trees at wolf's mouth height. *Thank goodness.* Then we were pounding downhill once more. I tried to keep closer to the taped circle this time.

Soon, the werewolves and I passed Kath, Ron and the djinn again. Ron's wave was smaller now, but the elementals were glowing dark red, rather than the fiery golden white they'd been before. The djinn didn't seem any different, though he'd given up hurling insults.

Kath had the grimoire in her tongs and was holding it over the point where the duct tape circle was joined, the same way I'd hold a marshmallow over a fire. I wondered what on Gaia she was trying to do, but didn't stop to ask.

"Once more round and you're done," she encouraged. I didn't know how she could bear to stand so close to the elementals. It was hot enough running around them, let alone standing so cosily close. I grunted in acknowledgement. I wasn't usually a grunter, but that was all I could manage. I was fit for dog-walking, not for running with the wolves.

The last uphill run was harder than the first two. I was tiring, and it showed in slips and stumbles. Somehow, I found a rabbit hole with my foot again. I tripped and sprawled full length, my outflung hands actually touching the salt-covered duct tape. I hadn't begun to recover myself when one of the elementals was right there, poised and waiting for me to break the circle. The heat of it was intense. Just inside the circle, directly beneath the elemental, I saw someone's discarded beer can melt and trickle downhill in little zigzags. It was astonishing that the duct tape still held together under such conditions. Surely it too should be melting? It was hot to the touch, and rough from the salt on its sticky surface.

"Back," said a voice in my ear. "Careful."

Out of the corner of my eye I saw that it was the blond werewolf. I didn't need telling. Before I could growl my annoyance at him, he disappeared. Feeling abandoned, but determined not to release these elementals back into the world, I wriggled into a kneeling position, closer to the flames but not sprawled on the forest floor. At least I didn't feel quite so helpless that way.

Moving slowly, for fear that I'd disperse the salt off the tape and break the circle, I eased first one finger, then another, then another, off the sticky surface. The tape tore along the edge as I pried my ring finger free. It was all I could do not to jump up and run away as the elemental leered closer, like a flame veering in the wind. My right hand was free. I felt in my pocket for the extra salt, but it must have fallen out during one of my stumbles.

The middle finger of my left hand was almost over the edge of the tape. I felt my skin blistering as the elemental edged closer, but I was terrified that I'd let it out if I removed my fingers too fast. I'd already seen how easily the duct tape tore. Not to mention the damage an uncontained elemental could do.

There was going to be a gap in the salt as soon as I got my hand off the tape. I needed that extra salt, but it could be anywhere in the circle I'd been running. What could I do now? The three circles weren't complete, and I was unable to move without tearing the salted circle which held the elementals in place. If I moved, they'd get me, and after me, everyone else. I let my forehead sink to the warm, spikey, pine-scented forest floor. I was done for.

Chapter Eight

THRICE ROUND WIDDERSHINS

A hairy hand thrust its way into my field of vision. It was holding an open packet of salt like the ones Kath had been using. The werewolf must have run back along our path to find it. That superior sense of smell had to have come into play for him to find the salt so quickly. Perhaps those doglike traits weren't so bad after all.

"Thanks," I said, taking the proffered salt packet in my free hand.

"Move, then pour. Fast." The blond werewolf practically barked the instruction, but I didn't need to be told twice. I ripped my finger away from the hot tape, which tore as I'd feared it would. But as the elemental blazed with a greedy roar towards the tiny gap, I dumped the contents of the salt packet onto the tape. The gap filled once again, and the elemental butted up against it like a lava flow meeting the sea.

The werewolf offered me a hand to help me to my feet, which I ignored. My hands were sore enough already. He shrugged and stepped aside with a gesture as though to wave me into a fancy dining room. As I began my dash uphill again, I saw the fast-moving bodies of the other werewolves in flashes through the tree trunks. The smoke was still thick, but a stiff breeze sprang up as we ran, beginning to clear it.

I rounded the top of the circle and thudded downhill, around, and back to Kath, Ron and the djinn.

"Three times round," I gasped out.

"That'll do," Kath said. She looked at me all too sharply for an old woman. "Burnt your hand, did you?" Without waiting for an answer, Kath slapped my sore hand onto the grimoire which she still held in her tongs.

I gave an involuntary shriek, expecting to be burnt even more since she'd been holding it near the elementals. But the grimoire was icy cold. I pushed my hand against it as though doing so would make my scorched skin sink into the cover for greater relief. Sadly, magical or no, it was still a book. My hand didn't move, but the cool feeling of its smooth exterior soothed me.

As my hand cooled, the elementals seemed to shrink in on themselves. At first a whirling tornado of fire in the treetops, raining burning branches and pine needles, they quickly morphed into several balls of fire whipping to and fro, still roaring. Then they were balls of sparks, glowing less and less. The sound reduced to crackling and spitting. Then there was nothing left but blackened trees and the stench of quenched bushfire: smoke, scorched earth, overheated pine oil and a lingering warmth in the air. The roaring of the elementals still echoed in my mind, but in the real world everything was silent.

The werewolves milled around nearby, reminding me somehow of my family's dogs when someone forgot to give praise when praise was due. I gave the blond one a weak smile. "Thanks for helping me back there," I told him.

"Yes, well done, boys. You might as well head back now," Kath said.

The werewolf gave a short nod, and he and the rest of the werewolves loped off downhill in the direction of the bus.

"Is that it then?" I asked when I'd got over the shock of the chilly grimoire and the abrupt departure of the elementals. Were there embers still glowing in the depths of the circle? I couldn't be sure. My eyes still watered and stung. "Are they gone?"

"But of course they are," the djinn said, billowing towards me. "Once they were fully contained I banished them to the plane they came from, naturally."

Kath shot him a glare, and he hastily added,

"With a little help from the circle magic, of course. And that book." The glare *he* sent at the grimoire made me wonder if Ron had somehow used it to become the djinn's carrier. But the djinn kept on talking, bringing me back to the present.

"The question is, what let them come here?"

"What do you mean?" I asked, uneasily.

Ron shambled towards us. He looked exhausted, even more so than I felt. His wrinkled skin was more wizened than it had been, as though he was wrung dry. "He means, elementals shouldn't pop up in the bush like this. They usually need a spark to set them off. Although it does happen more than people realise. What do you think, Kath?"

The tension between the old couple seemed to have disappeared. Kath handed me the grimoire and taking a moment to rummage in her bulky bag, pulled out a large thermos flask.

"Tea, Ron?" she asked. She unscrewed the lid and poured amber liquid into the thermos cup without waiting for an answer.

"Thanks." Ron drank the proffered tea in one long gulp and handed the cup back.

"I think," Kath said slowly, "That we'd better find out where that dragon headed. We're still close to Rotorua, and it did fly in this direction. Perhaps it was more annoyed with the pie than they usually are." She didn't seem apologetic, and to be honest, I didn't blame her. I hadn't wanted to be eaten by a dragon. "I shouldn't have sent those werewolves back," she muttered, apparently to herself. "You didn't happen to spot a dragon while you ran the circles, did you?" Kath looked at me.

I shook my head. "I had a hard enough time just running. I nearly broke through the circle by accident," I admitted. "The only thing I saw was an empty can of beer."

Ron snapped his fingers.

"That'll be it. Probably some fool teenagers mucking about in the bush with lighters or some such. No need to look for dragons when there's humans to blame."

I wasn't sure if he was joking or not, but it did seem unlikely that a dragon had dropped the beer can I'd seen.

"Did the elementals not cause the fire then?" I asked, confused.

"Not on their own," Ron informed me. "They only get through when someone weakens things from this side."

I nodded my understanding. "The beer can melted," I told him. I was still spooked by how close I'd come to annihilation.

"No chance of fingerprints, then." Kath seemed disappointed.

"I'll look around, shall I?" the djinn said.

"Do that," Kath told him.

But it wasn't until Ron added, "Yes, please do take a look. We need to make sure they're too scared to do it again," that the djinn wafted into the air, winding around tree trunks until he was mostly out of sight.

Kath put the thermos away and crossed her arms, looking put out. "I still think that dragon might have caused this," she said.

"Do dragons often let elementals through?" I asked. I knew the theory, but it seemed like these two had much more experience than the accounts I'd read.

"They're drawn to the thin zones," Ron said. He sounded indulgent. Clearly, he had a soft spot for dragons.

"Thin, *hot* zones," Kath said reprovingly. "No-one's proved that dragons cause tears between planes," she added. "But it's likely."

"No more likely than a mundane cause," Ron protested. This sounded like an old argument. Luckily, the djinn returned at that point, his thin purple trail of smoke thickening until he once again formed a more-or-less person-sized cloud.

"No sign of dragons... now. But three young hooligans in a scorched looking car are driving away rather fast down the farm road towards town," the djinn reported. "Their driving skills seem very much lacking. And there are the remains of a campfire uphill from here." He shook his smoky head. "*Very* messy."

"There, you see?" Ron almost cackled in triumph at his theory being proven right.

"That's still not proof, you old fool," Kath argued. "They might have been upset by the dragon landing in their camp."

"Well, perhaps," Ron agreed. "In which case, they'll have gotten the fright they deserve for mucking about. Let's wrap things up here. We've got a cruise to catch in case you've forgotten."

Kath brightened immediately.

"Good point, Ron. That dragon will be much happier in the hills anyway. And the elementals we sent back today won't be in any shape to try another incursion for a few years yet. Let's be going." Kath turned to me. "Hand feeling better? Righto, I'm ready for a kip on that bus."

Chapter Nine

A DIFFERENT KIND OF FORTUNE

The bus driver was touchingly glad to see us return, although the other passengers muttered a bit about the smoky smell that clung to us. I didn't care; I was so happy to see the agreeably normal interior of that bus, worn seats, loud fellow passengers and all. Compared to a burning forest, it felt homely and comfortable. Several passengers were hanging around on the grassy roadside, including the blue-singleted team and their coach. Some of the team were doing press-ups; I wondered why none of them had volunteered to come. They looked young and athletic enough to have run circles around elementals with much more ease than I had done.

"I think I'm seeking a slightly less physical fortune than saving the world," I said, partly to Kath, partly to myself. I offered the old lady a hand up onto the bus; to my surprise, she took it.

"But you did so well, dear. Are you sure?" Kath asked as she settled herself into her seat beside me. She paused to give Ron a quick hand-squeeze as the wizard passed by on his way to his own seat nearer the back. The djinn was nowhere in sight, but Ron was carrying his bag, where the djinn was presumably hiding away again. I looked at their clasped, knobbly hands, and wondered at the intimacy that simple gesture conveyed. Ron gave Kath a smile and continued, the moment lost in the kerfuffle of boarding.

"I'm sure," I said firmly. I wanted the chance to find myself; find something I was good at; maybe even find some sort of relationship. Mostly though, I just wanted to be somewhere that wasn't my home town. Saving the world — or at least a small part of it — from an elemental incursion was certainly an adrenaline rush, but it wasn't what I wanted to be doing every day. "I think I'm looking for something more... bookish," I added, thinking of the long hours I'd poured into study over the years. The study itself hadn't been hard. Just lonely. "Though I do like meeting new people."

"That's good to know, dear," Kath said as the bus lurched into motion once more. "You know, I think I'll go have a little chat with Ron before my kip after all." She heaved herself to her feet then paused, looking at her heavy bag. "You can look after my bag for a few more minutes."

It was a statement, not a request, but I didn't mind too much. It wasn't like I was going to be doing anything other than sitting down. Even the thin padding of the bus seat felt luxurious after my efforts in the boulder country. I watched the forest flicker past the window until the trees were superseded by vast, flat, grassy plains. The road improved as we crossed the plains, getting wider and smoother.

We paused for another rest stop in the inland city of Hamilton, Kirikiriroa, not far from a wide river, but I stayed on the bus this time. No sense in risking another strange encounter. Besides, I liked the idea of being near the sea for a change. As we left the riverside city, I felt myself relax as the possibility of deadly corners receded. Growing bored with grassy fields and cows, I checked my phone; I had just enough bars of coverage to do an internet search. Now I knew in which city I was going to be seeking my fortune, I'd need somewhere to stay. I should really have started looking as soon as I got on the bus, but I'd been distracted.

My search for a hostel that had single rooms, not only dorms (I'd decided I was too old for a dorm room, before seeing the price of single rooms) was not going well. Every single room I'd found so far had been well above my price range. I had savings, but I'd woefully underestimated the cost of rent in a big city. Perhaps I'd have to relax my expectations after all. I wrinkled my nose at the thought. I wasn't fresh out of school, to relish the thought of sharing a room with some stranger.

I looked up when Kath returned from the back of the bus. There hadn't been any djinn-like wafts of smoke investigating her bag this time; perhaps the djinn had lost interest now he knew what was in it.

"Do you live in Auckland?" I asked Kath when she heaved herself into the empty seat beside me.

"'Course I do. Why else would me and Ron be taking the bus back there otherwise?" she said.

"I thought you might be visiting that niece you mentioned," I said. "But I'm asking because I need a tip on a good, cheap place to stay. All I can find is backpackers' hostels or five star hotels. Hotels are too expensive, and hostels are too crow— cheap."

Kath laughed uproariously at my hasty rephrase, drawing the eyes of the whole bus.

"Crow-cheap indeed," she gasped at long last. "Lucky thing there's no crows in this country. But you do look a little old to be sharing a bunk bed. As a matter of fact, there are some middle-of-the road places here and there. And we *are* just coming back to catch a cruise ship. It's time for us to retire and go see the islands," Kath said smugly. "But how about I tell you what Ron and me were just talking about, and *then* you worry about somewhere to stay."

"Alright," I said cautiously. Given the dragon and the elementals, I had no idea what Kath and her wizard husband could have been discussing.

Kath rummaged around in her bag long enough to find a crochet hook and a skein of wool, which she began looping into a chain before she started talking again. I eyed the growing chain warily. Some mages are said to make spells with yarn. But as far as I could tell from a few minutes' observation, Kath was just making a hat. Perhaps she wanted one to match her husband's.

"It's like this," she said at last. "Me and Ron have had enough of looking after our business. It's going well, mind you, but we've got that cruise to do, krakens to visit, that kind of thing, and we don't really fancy coming back to work afterwards."

I looked at her blankly. I'd sort-of gathered that Ron and Kath had a bookshop, but they hadn't told me anything about it, unless you counted

Ron's comment about renovation. Why was she telling *me* they wanted to move on?

Kath saw my carefully polite expression and cackled.

"You're perfect for the role," she said.

"What role?"

She put her growing disc of crocheted wool onto her lap long enough to pat my shoulder, as though I was a rather foolish toddler. "You look like the sort of young lady who's just itching to take on a magical bookshop," she said.

"You want me to look after your magical bookshop?" I gasped in astonishment.

"No, dear, we want you to take it over. So long as you keep the bookshop running, it and the apartment above it is yours." Kath's tone was matter of fact.

"But — I thought you had a niece who was looking after it?" I couldn't quite believe my good fortune.

"Pah! She told us years ago she wasn't having anything to do with the bookshop. No, she runs a dragon sanctuary in the mountains down south. We've just come back from a visit. The bookshop's closed right now."

"You're sure?" I asked again.

"Surer than you'll ever be!" Kath cackled at her own joke. "We want to live a little, see the world," she said when she'd regained her breath. "There's more to life than selling books and having an occasional stay in the hot springs with Laura. Besides, I always have to share the water with a dragon there. I hear they have quite different problems in the islands." She beamed at me.

"Like elemental incursions?" I asked drily.

"Yes, that sort of thing, dear. Much more suited to my time of life, don't you think?"

I hardly knew what to say, but I knew I couldn't pass up an offer that good.

Chapter Ten

THE BOOKSHOP

The bus crested the harbour bridge and slid to a halt just off the motorway, in a somewhat desolate bus station next to a reclaimed sports field and an expanse of mangroves. The other occupants of the bus dispersed in various directions when we finally arrived. The sports team jogged off towards the field, all vim and vigour despite the long journey. The werewolves turned in the direction of a patch of bush that rose up beside the motorway. When I looked around for the vampire, he was nowhere to be seen. Perhaps he was hiding under the seats until darkness fell. Or perhaps he left the bus back in Hamilton.

Kath, Ron and the leprechauns all headed in the direction of a local bus. The last I saw of the leprechauns was them asking riddles of another bus driver, who looked perplexed. "You can't pay for a bus fare with riddles," he argued.

I silently wished him luck and followed Kath and Ron towards another bus. This one was labelled 'Woodside'.

"Just pay for one stage, dear," Kath advised me, as she paid for herself. I noticed that Ron only paid for one person, too. The djinn was keeping out of sight. That seemed a little underhanded – but then again, the djinn didn't take up his own seat, so perhaps it was reasonable.

The journey was short and uneventful, though my eyes were wide as I took in the new sights and sounds of the city. A volcano caught my attention out in the harbour, but we headed away from that, up a steep but short hill. We drove across the motorway and past the bush – werewolf tails just now disappearing into the trees – and then over a couple of rolling hills smothered with mismatched houses, all angled to get the best possible view of the harbour. Then we passed some more bush, some more sports fields, more houses all together than I'd seen in my life, and a small mall with shops clustered around it, before Kath tapped my shoulder again.

"Press the button, dear," she told me. "It's our stop."

"I'll stay on and get the bags from home," Ron said. "Don't be long."

Kath gave him a nod, and we disembarked onto a windy street with street trees surrounded by paving stones. She led the way to an unmarked, peeling blue door sandwiched between a closed second-hand store and a noodle shop, also closed, although a sign on its door promised it would be opening later.

I found the letter with my name on it waiting for me on the mat behind the front door of the bookshop. It had clearly been there for a while since a few leaves had also blown in on top of it.

I recognised my sister's handwriting at once and stuffed it into my pocket. No way was I letting my seer family spoil this moment for me.

"Anything interesting there, dear?" Kath asked inquisitively.

I felt my cheeks heating in embarrassment. "Nothing important," I said. "Give me the full tour, please."

She gave me a knowing glance, but smiled a little and led the way inside, flicking a light switch on by the door as she did so.

The smell of books gusted over me. Old, new, treasured or trash, it looked like this place held the full range.

"The scrolls have their own room over here," she said, pulling aside a velvet curtain that must block most of what little light there was. There didn't seem to be any windows. Just row upon row of bookshelves. The scrolls were neatly arranged in pigeonholes, with careful, old-fashioned letters stuck in front of each slot. "Alphabetically arranged by the author, of course," she added. "Except where the author has inconveniently forgotten to sign his or her own spellwork, then we're forced to go by title or first word."

She closed the curtain again before I could examine the scrolls more closely and led the way to the old wooden desk which held an ancient cash register. She tapped it. "You'll probably want to upgrade, but not to worry if not. You'll need to be prepared to accept all sorts of payment types. You'll find many customers are set in their ways anyway." She cackled. "Just like Ron and me. Now, excuse me if I don't show you upstairs. I don't fancy coming down them again, not after that excitement with the elementals. It's got a good view, though, not like down here. But the books have to be protected." She took my arm. "So, what do you think? Is it going to work?"

I snorted a little. "You know I'm not a seer. So, I don't know if it will or not. But I think I would definitely like to have a go at making it work."

The bookshop already felt like it could be my home. Sure, I'd make changes, put my own stamp on things. But running a magical bookshop? That was like winning the lottery. I hadn't dreamed of doing any such thing when I set out to seek my fortune, but it felt like I'd landed on my feet.

Kath grinned at me, eyes twinkling ever so slightly. "That's the spirit, girl. Now, Ron's going to be getting impatient, and when he gets impatient, he lets that djinn loose, so I'd best be off. Besides, the cruise ship's in harbour and I want to be sure he got us a berth with a view."

I smiled back. "I'm sure you'll fix it if he hasn't," I said.

"You know it, dear. Righto, I'm off," she said. Without a backwards glance, she walked out of the shop. Her bag seemed less full than any other time I'd seen it. She seemed almost to grow taller as she stepped through the doorway, as though some great weight had been lifted from her shoulders.

I turned back to the bookshelves. I'd need to catalogue everything. And there was a lot more exploring to do. I hadn't seen the promised apartment upstairs yet, let alone perused all the bookshelves. My feet took me to the back of the bookstore first. It turned out there was a whole shelf of grimoires there. One of them had a very familiar cover. It looked like I had myself a book, a job, and a place to stay. I had found my fortune.

It wasn't until much later that night, while I was sitting on the sofa in the apartment over the bookshop, marvelling at how things had turned out and wondering exactly *how* to run a magical bookstore, that I remembered the letter. I pulled it from my pocket and smoothed out the crumples. Still, I hesitated a moment before opening it. Did I want my life to be dictated by seers? Absolutely not. But curiosity got the better of me. I tore it open. The smell of Delphine's favourite perfume wafted from the single piece of paper inside.

"Dear Sibyl," I read. "If you're reading this, you made it past the bus driver, the dragon, and the elementals. Relax! You've got a few years to enjoy your bookshop before things get interesting again. Don't forget to stock up on hamster food. Love, Delphine."

The letter was dated several days before I'd left home. I shook my head. Typical seer missive, claiming knowledge of things they hadn't been around for, and giving vaguely mysterious hints for the future. Still, it looked as if I was on my own, just as I had wanted.

I crumpled up the letter and tossed it towards the waste paper bin I'd found by the desk at the other end of the room. I missed, but not by much. Ignoring it for now, I headed to the kitchen to make myself a drink. It was time to settle in and enjoy myself.

Afterword

Thank you for reading the first book in my Woodside Cosy series. If you enjoyed it, please consider leaving a review so other people know it's worth a shot! It was a blast to write a fantasy story set in the country I grew up in, and I'm looking forward to writing more in this series.

Sign up to my monthly newsletter at https://www.melissagunn.com to find out what the werewolves do while Sibyl is running circles in the bush.

This book was inspired by an actual bus trip that was much less eventful than the one described!

Most of the locations mentioned you'll find on a map of Aotearoa New Zealand, but probably not Woodside; although it's based on a real suburb of Auckland/Tāmaki Makaurau, the name comes from the historical records of the area.

Also by Melissa Gunn

Weather Gods series:

Flash Flood

Storm Surge

Heat Wave

Short stories & novellas:

Treescape (First published in Magic and Mystery:

A limited Edition Urban Fantasy Mystery Anthology)

Feels Like Heaven (in Aftermath: Stories of Survival in Aotearoa New Zealand)

First Pav on Mars (in Pav Deconstructed, Pavlova Press)

A Gift of Coconuts (Imagine 2200 2024 collection)

Acknowledgements

Thanks to the Writer's Cafe Novel Writers Club for feedback on early drafts; my critique group for being helpfully critical and to Grace Bridges for editing (any remaining mistakes are my own), to Alana for helpful location photos, to Élise for proofreading & critiques, and of course to all my family for putting up with my many writing meetings and random conversations.

www.ingramcontent.com/pod-product-compliance
Lightning Source LLC
Chambersburg PA
CBHW031259060726
47590CB00003B/973